A Michael Neugebauer Book

Copyright © 1981 by Neugebauer Press, Salzburg.

Published by Picture Book Studio, Saxonville, MA.

Distributed in the United States by Simon & Schuster.

Distributed in Canada by Vanwell Publishing, St. Catharines, Ontario.

All rights reserved. Printed in Hong Kong.

10 9 8 7 6 5 4 3 2 1

Library of Congress Cataloging-in-Publication Data

Gantschev, Ivan

[Mondsee. English]

The moon lake / Ivan Gantschev.

p. cm. — (Pixies ; #24)

Translation of: Der Mondsee.

Summary: A shepherd boy follows a lost sheep to the secret lake in which the moon bathes, but greedy townspeople soon learn that its banks are encrusted with silver, gold, and precious jewels.

ISBN 0-88708-304-8 : $4.95

[1. Shepherds—Fiction. 2. Lakes—Fiction. 3.Greed—Fiction.]

I. Title. II. Series.

PZ7.G15336Mo   1993

[E]—dc 19 —dc20   92-36646

CIP

AC

THE MOON LAKE

Ivan Gantschev

Picture Book Studio

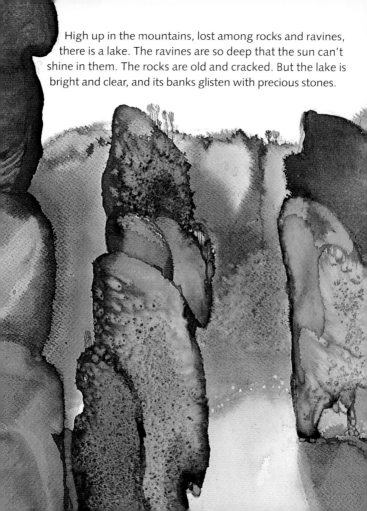

High up in the mountains, lost among rocks and ravines, there is a lake. The ravines are so deep that the sun can't shine in them. The rocks are old and cracked. But the lake is bright and clear, and its banks glisten with precious stones.

People say that sometimes the moon comes to visit the earth. And as she comes slowly down, she always heads for the icy lake where she likes to bathe. After she has had her bath she shakes herself dry, showering the banks of the lake with precious jewels, with gold-dust and with silver. So people call the lake Moon Lake, although no one knows where it is. Many people have searched for it, but always in vain. They set out full of hope and pride, and return forlorn. Some never do return, but are lost forever in rocky wilderness.

Only one person knew the lake: a quiet old shepherd. Who could he have told about it? He lived in the mountains with his sheep, far from any towns or villages. It took a day and a night travelling to reach his cottage through thick forests, over hills, and down deep valleys. And who would go through all that trouble? So he lived in his lonely cottage, with only his grandson Peter to keep him company. The years came and went and the shepherd grew older and older.

In winter, the paths were blocked by snow.
The old shepherd stayed inside keeping warm
by the fire and Peter looked after him.

"I've always wanted to show my grandson the Moon
Lake," thought the old man. "He might like those
beautiful stones." But he wasn't strong enough
to take the boy into the mountains. When
the old man died, Peter buried him
close to the cottage. And so the
shepherd took his secret with
him to the grave.

Peter stayed in the cottage on his own and looked after the sheep. And he was very happy. The sheep gave plenty of milk and he used some of it to make cheese which he could sell when he went to town. He didn't make the journey very often, but when he did, he bought salt for himself and the animals. He used wild apples, pears and raspberries to make jam for the winter. And in the garden he planted onions, beans, and lettuces.

One evening, when he was driving the sheep into their fold, he noticed that one of them was missing.

Peter took some bread, a piece of cheese and a few onions, and set out to look for the sheep. It was beginning to get dark when Peter came to a deep ravine. He thought he could hear a faint, helpless bleating coming from the bottom. So he lay on the cliff-edge and peered down. Far beneath him he saw a glistening lake, and on its bank, looking small and lost, was his sheep, bleating piteously up at him. Peter found a passage between the rocks and climbed down. When he reached the bottom, the moon was out, and he could see as clearly as by day.

All around the lake, everything was shining and sparkling. The banks were covered in jewels! He liked them so much that he began picking up the biggest and the most beautiful ones, and putting them in his shepherd's sack.

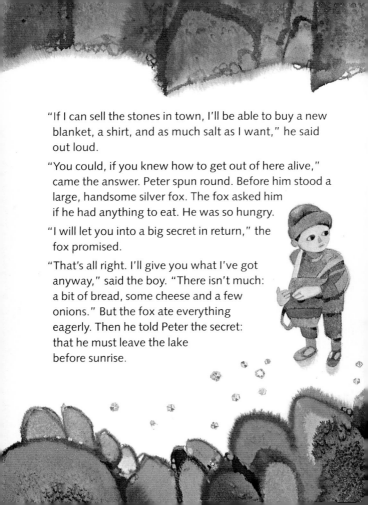

"If I can sell the stones in town, I'll be able to buy a new blanket, a shirt, and as much salt as I want," he said out loud.

"You could, if you knew how to get out of here alive," came the answer. Peter spun round. Before him stood a large, handsome silver fox. The fox asked him if he had anything to eat. He was so hungry.

"I will let you into a big secret in return," the fox promised.

"That's all right. I'll give you what I've got anyway," said the boy. "There isn't much: a bit of bread, some cheese and a few onions." But the fox ate everything eagerly. Then he told Peter the secret: that he must leave the lake before sunrise.

"When the sun rises," said the fox, "you will be blinded by the dazzling stones, and you will never find your way home. Come with me, and I'll show you the way to the top." Peter heaved the sheep onto his shoulder. With the fox's help, he was soon out of the ravine, and there he said goodbye to his new friend. By sunrise, he was safely back at the cottage with his sheep.

A few days later, Peter made the journey into town. He spread out his stones on a cloth in the marketplace and put them up for sale. But then a terrible thing happened.

Two policemen came and ordered him to follow them. They took him to the castle of an important minister. He was with the police chief, waiting for the young shepherd, and they demanded to know where Peter had gotten the precious stones. The boy told them his story, but they just laughed and took the stones from him. Peter was powerless to stop them.

Then the minister wanted to know how to find the lake, but it was difficult for Peter to explain. The police chief threatened to throw Peter down the deepest well, full of snakes and frogs.

So Peter agreed to lead the men to the lake. The minister took two other friends with him, and they all set off. They rode through the darkness of the night along the tracks which Peter showed them.

From time to time the men let him ride with them on one of the horses, since they were in a hurry. A night and a day had passed when they reached the ravine.

The moon rose as before, the banks of the lake glistened, and the men eagerly started cramming the jewels into their sacks.

Then Peter remembered the fox's advice. "Excuse me sir," he said to the minister, "we must leave here before sunrise or we'll all be blinded."

But the minister just replied angrily: "Go away, you stupid little shepherd boy!" and he boxed the boy's ears.

So Peter slipped away without saying another word, and left the police chief, the minister and his friends by the lake, busily collecting jewels.

When the sun rose, the men were blinded by the dazzling stones. Weighed down by their full sacks, they wandered among the rocks until they fell into the deep ravines.

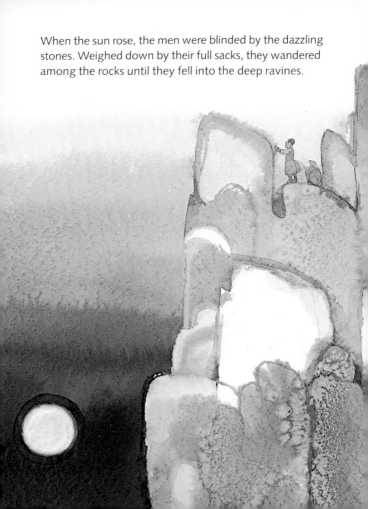